Grandma Bendy and the

Great Snake
Escape

CONTENTS

Boris   p. 15

Snake on the loose!   p. 30

Panic!   p. 45

The search continues   p. 63

The launch   p. 74

Mr. Brainfreeze's Ice   p. 86
Cream Parlour

The snake   p. 101

Back to normal... almost   p. 114

The diary of Spag Bol   p. 121

Meet the characters!

Well, it's only polite to introduce them to you before the story begins.

Introducing...

Grandma Bendy

She is no ordinary grandma, she is a super, stretchy, twisty, bendy grandma.

Can your grandma do that? OUCH! No, mine neither.

Spag Bol

Grandma Bendy's dog. Ahhh, isn't he cute.

Max and Lucy

The grandchildren. Well Grandma Bendy wouldn't be a grandma without these two scallywags.

Mike Grimace

Um, you might want to stay clear of him, he's the school bully.

Lady Lavender

She is very snooty. She always wears a hat. Does she have hair underneath? Who knows?!

Sergeant Nevil Rodent

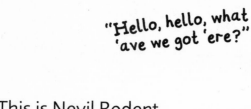

"Hello, hello, what 'ave we got 'ere?"

This is Nevil Rodent, he's the Police officer. He likes eating jam sandwiches.

Mr Brain Freeze

He's the ice cream shop owner; look at his hair!

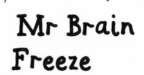

Val Crowe

She's the shopkeeper and she loves to run everywhere.

Miss Letterbury

Is a teacher at Horace Hicks First School.

Suzy Valentine

She is a writer and photographer for the Pumperton Newspaper.

Welcome to

As you can see, Pumperton is quite small, but that

Pumperton!

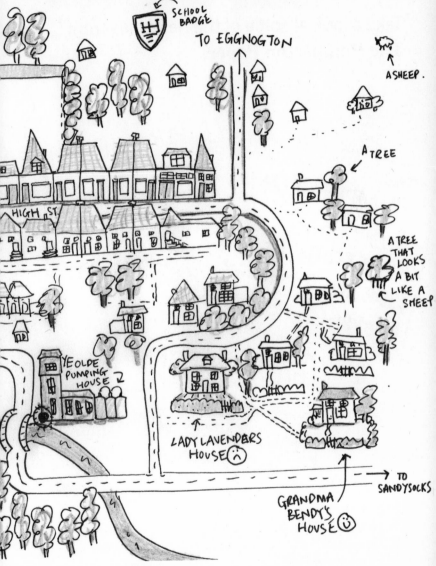

doesn't mean **BIG** things don't happen here.

Take a look at some of the headlines from **The Pumperton Paper**:

THE PUMPERTON PAPER

ROLLERCOASTER RIDE IN RUNAWAY SHOPPING TROLLE

THE PUMPERTON PAPER

FEARED ESCAPED TIGER JUST SOMEONE'S CAT

THE PUMPERTON PAPER

GALE FORCE WINDS BLOW SANTA'S BEARD OFF

THE
PUMPERTON
PAPER

STICK INSECT
STUCK INSIDE
JAM SANDWICH

THE
PUMPERTON
PAPER

FARMS MISSING
COWS FOUND IN
ICE-CREAM
PARLOUR

THE
PUMPERTON
PAPER

IS A BLACK
PANTHER PROWLING
IN PUMPERTON?

THE
PUMPERTON
PAPER

PUMPERTONS
TED BARROW CROWNED
MARROW CHAMPION
AGAIN!

See, there is always something happening
here and today looks no different...

Boris

Miss Letterbury stood in front of class 4B trying to calm them down, there was a lot of excitement surrounding the hamster Jake had brought in for show and tell.

"4B sit down, stop chattering, Mrs Bottomly might have let you climb on the desks like monkeys, but in my class we sit at our desks nicely."

The children all scrambled into their seats and were quiet, except

for Jake's hamster, who squeaked occasionally in his cage.

"Now, as you know, our first lesson will be Show and Tell and I can't wait to hear what delights you all got up to over the holidays! Who would like to start us off?" asked Miss Letterbury.

Lucy was feeling pretty nervous about

Miss Letterbury 16
she's pretty nice →

speaking in front of everyone and was keen to get it over with before she got even more nervous. She waved her hand in the air to get Miss Letterbury's attention.

"Ah, yes, Lucy, isn't it? Have you brought in your show and tell?"

"Yes Miss," said Lucy, "It's in my bag Miss...."

Mike, Horace Hicks' very own school bully, was sitting behind Lucy and he was bored. He looked across at Lucy's bag on the floor and realised it was right next to his... and it was open. A big naughty grin crept across his face as an idea popped into his head...

"BORIS!"

Mike made sure no-one was looking then leaned over and unzipped his school bag. He reached inside and grabbed something from it and in one swift movement placed it into Lucy's bag.

"Gotcha!" he whispered to himself, then sat back in his chair with a grin on his face. Nobody had noticed a thing.

"A surprise, how fantastic, well you can definitely go first!" Miss Letterbury said, "We like surprises, don't we class 4B?" Class 4B nodded sleepily.

Lucy picked up her bag and walked to the front of the class.

"The best thing about my summer holidays, was my grandma," said Lucy proudly.

Mike groaned, "Another boring story about someone's boring grandma!" he said under his breath.

"Mike, don't be so rude," snapped Miss Letterbury who had overheard him.

Lucy now feeling more nervous, tried not to look at Mike, instead she took a deep breath.

"My grandma, isn't really like other people's grandmas," Lucy continued, "she's really funny, she can skip, do star jumps, slide down the stairs and she is really bendy. She can twizzle her arms in all directions AND she can even do the splits! My brother and I call her Grandma Bendy and her favourite thing to wear is stripey jumpers and leggings," said Lucy.

"If she's really that bendy, is she in your bag?" jeered Mike from the back of the class.

"Mike Grimace, will you be quiet," said Miss Letterbury.

"Of course she's not IN my bag!" said Lucy glaring at Mike, "In my bag is a...

Aaahhhh !"

Lucy screamed and her arm shot up in the air, jiggling up and down like she was doing some sort of wiggly dance.

Mike, who had been waiting for this moment, started chuckling to himself.

"Heee hee ha haaa," his chuckle turned to laughter, then his laughter turned into snorting, like a pig!

"Ha ha haaa SNORT SNORT ha ha."

"Michael James Grimace, that is quite enough, stop it at once. Lucy, is that an impression of your grandma's twizzly arms?" asked Miss Letterbury, "I think that's a very clever thing to bring in and show us," she said.

"Nooooo Miss.... aargh, there's something up my... up my..." Lucy was wiggling her arm around and around in all directions, "there's

something up my jumper,
Miss!"

Suddenly the
'something' flew out
of Lucy's jumper. It was

something long,

    something green,

something stripey

    and something wriggly

and it fell onto the floor, in front of the whole
class.

"Ha ha ha, is it one of your grandma's stripey
jumpers?" laughed Mike.

Lucy jumped back
and screamed. Then the
twenty-two other children in class
4B jumped back and screamed.

Then Miss Letterbury screamed,
"Aaaaaaaaaaaahhhhhhh!

IT'S A SNAKE!!!"

and they all ran to the back of the classroom.

Mike stood up, still laughing and walked
casually towards the snake.

"Ha ha ha, it's just Boris!" said
Mike and he bent down to pick
him up, but Boris darted off
towards the desks.

"Boris, no!" shouted Mike.

Boris was now slithering across Ali's desk directly towards the basket of apples he'd picked from his apple tree at home and Boris must have been hungry because he gobbled them all up!

He then wriggled over to Suki's desk, who had brought in her collection of bouncy balls and Boris ate them too!

He then started to slink his way towards Jake's hamster cage.

"Nooo, not my hamster!" shouted Jake from the back of the class in horror.

eek!

Everyone gasped, some children covered their eyes, they couldn't bear to look. Boris slid right up to the bars of the cage and just as Mike lunged to grab him he tripped and fell onto the desk, knocking the cage over and sending Boris flying up into the air.

Everyone held their breath, terrified of where the snake would land.

The snake twirled in the air and began to fall back down to the floor where... it bounced.

And bounced,
   and bounced
      all around the room.

The children and Miss Letterbury watched in amazement as Boris spat up the bouncy balls he'd swallowed and wriggled, dazed, out of the door and down the hall.

Miss Letterbury ran towards the classroom door, but there was no snake to be seen. "Oh no!" she said to herself, "Where can it have gone?" But she soon knew exactly where Boris had wriggled off to when a scream echoed down the corridor.

"Aaaaahhhhhh snake!"

He had slithered into the worst place he could have slithered…

Mrs. McDotty
THE HEADTEACHER HHFS

Ten minutes of screaming later and with no idea where the snake had now disappeared to, Mrs McDotty closed Horace Hicks First School and sent everyone home, everyone except Lucy.

Lucy sat with Police Sergeant Nevil Rodent who had been called to the school to investigate.

"But it wasn't me!" Lucy pleaded to the Sergeant, "I didn't bring a snake into school! I brought some pictures of me, Max and Grandma Bendy! See, here we are at Splashdown Park and this is one of us as pirates at Puffin Island, and this one..."

HORACE HICKS
1887 FOUNDER

Nevil Rodent interrupted her, "Snakes, puffins, parrots! What next? I think we've had quite enough wildlife from your backpack for one day, young lady! Now grab your brother, I'm taking you home."

Empty brain inside →

"Pirates, not parrots," whispered Lucy to herself, knowing there was little point in trying to explain anything to stupid Sergeant Nevil Rodent.

Snake on the loose!

Knock knock knock

"Grrrrrrroof, woof," barked Spag Bol. He knew exactly who was knocking at the door and jumped up at it in excitement.

"Ooh, scallywags, early scallywags!" said Grandma Bendy, surprised to hear Lucy and Max back from school so early. She stopped cleaning and went to open the door, but was shocked to see a Police Sergeant stood there with her grandchildren.

"Is everything okay?" asked Grandma Bendy anxiously, bouncing the feather duster in her hand.

"'Ello, 'ello, Mrs Bendy, I presume? Sergeant Nevil Rodent of the Pumperton Police, I hear you're looking after these two," he said, nodding at Lucy and Max.

"Yes, that's right, these scallywags are mine. Well, mine until their parents collect them after work," replied Grandma Bendy, "Are they okay?"

"They're fine," said the sergeant, "but there's been an incident at the school involving a snake and this one," he tapped Lucy on the head, "School's shut 'til further notice. Lucy and I have had a few words, but most of it was nonsense. No one's in trouble but they could be if this snake isn't found." And with that, he handed Lucy and Max over to Grandma Bendy, got into his police car and drove off.

Grandma Bendy was just about to shut the door when she spotted a pink hat peeping up from behind her neighbour's hedge.

"Oh no," she thought, "nosy Lady Lavender, she must have seen and heard everything!"

Lady Lavender was the nosiest person in Pumperton. She liked to listen to other people's conversations and gossip about it to everyone she met. Her favourite person to gossip to was Suzy Valentine, top news reporter at the local Pumperton newspaper.

she's SO nosy
she's probably noseying
on you reading this book!

If Lady Lavender overheard something, it wasn't long before the whole of Pumperton would be reading about it in the paper.

"Come on scallywags, inside quickly," said Grandma Bendy, shutting the door firmly behind them.

"It was Mike," said Max excitedly.

"Well," said Lucy, interrupting, "we think it was Mike. It certainly wasn't me even though everyone thinks it was."

"Even Miss Letterbury thinks it was

Lucy's snake," said Max quickly.

"We tried to catch it," Lucy chimed, "but no-one could, it ate Suki's bouncy balls and nearly Jake's hamster and it just kept bouncing and bouncing..."

"...and bouncing and bouncing," Max continued, "then..."

"Woah, woah, woah," Grandma Bendy stopped him, she was struggling to keep up, "s-l-o-w down, or you will both explode!"

"But it wasn't me!" interrupted Lucy again, breathless from talking too quickly.

"Children can burst from talking too fast," said Grandma Bendy. "POP! And they're gone, like a balloon filled with too much air. Now, sit down and I will make you both

- POP -

some fizz-floats and we will start again."

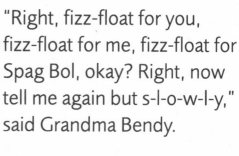
How to keep mum happy ☺

fizz float.

Grandma Bendy put the feather duster down, opened a bottle of home-made lemonade, added two strawberry jelly cubes, a scoop of Mr Brain Freeze's special raspberry whirl ice cream and a sprig of broccoli – to make sure she didn't get into trouble from Lucy and Max's mum for not giving them enough veggies.

"Right, fizz-float for you, fizz-float for me, fizz-float for Spag Bol, okay? Right, now tell me again but s-l-o-w-l-y," said Grandma Bendy.

SPAGBOL

"We think Mike brought a snake called Boris into school," began Lucy.

"Yeah, Boris..." repeated Max.

Lucy told Grandma Bendy every last little detail and Max helped by repeating most of what Lucy said.

"I see," said Grandma Bendy "a snake? A snake that is now on the loose, am I correct?" "Yes, eeek!" said Lucy realising how serious that sounded.

"Yeah, yikes!" said Max.

"Eek and yikes indeed!" said Grandma Bendy, "But if this snake was dangerous, you can bet this silly boy 'Mike' wouldn't have dared go near it, let alone bring it into school, so I think this snake must be pretty harmless!" said Bendy.

"Yelp!" said Spag Bol, who did not like the idea of a snake on the loose, harmless or not.

"Spag Bol, get your pen, it's list time and we need a plan," said Grandma Bendy. "We must catch the snake before anyone sees it and does, A. any harm to it, B. any harm to themselves and C. before the whole village starts to panic."

"Woof," agreed Spag Bol and he dived under a

cushion on the sofa and came out carrying a pen in his mouth. Grandma Bendy reached into a drawer and pulled out a map of Pumperton.

She took the pen then drew onto the map, "Okay, the snake left the school here, was last seen heading in this direction, which means we must look for the snake just around here."

She drew a big circle around most of Pumperton, then took a notebook from her pocket and wrote:

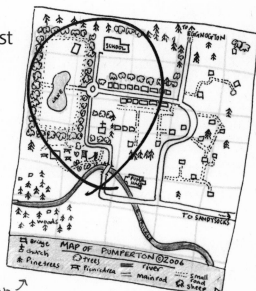

Ye Olde Map ↗
(from 2006)

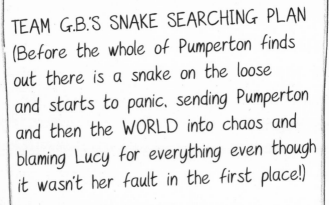

TEAM G.B.'S SNAKE SEARCHING PLAN
(Before the whole of Pumperton finds
out there is a snake on the loose
and starts to panic, sending Pumperton
and then the WORLD into chaos and
blaming Lucy for everything even though
it wasn't her fault in the first place!)

1. Val Crowe's Village Shop
2. The churchyard
3. The park
4. Mr. Brainfreeze's Ice Cream Parlour
5. THE REST OF THE WORLD!

Grandma Bendy had just finished the list,
when the letterbox rattled. She peered
around the kitchen door to see the Pumperton
Paper lying on the doormat. "Oh no."

Spag Bol ran down the hallway, picked up the paper and brought it back wagging his tail.

Grandma Bendy placed it on the kitchen table so everyone could see the headline:

THE PUMPERTON PAPER

Deadly snake on the loose in Pumperton

Deadly snake escapes in classroom. Horace Hicks First School shut down. Class 4B girl (who cannot be named for legal reasons, but has a brother at the school, blonde hair and a grandma nearby) is main suspect. Witnesses say girl kept snake in her school bag, waiting to scare teachers and school friends. Police involved. Public warned - do not approach. Public warned - snake will eat anything in its path.

EMERGENCY SNAKE HOTLINE
05555 555 555

42

"Oh no," said Lucy, "that's not true."

"Absolute flubberygubble, I knew Lady Lavender was being nosy! I bet she phoned that awful reporter Suzy Valentine as soon as Sergeant Rodent left and told her everything," said Grandma Bendy angrily.

"Grrr, woof," agreed Spag Bol.

"Right," Grandma Bendy calmed herself down, "let's put this plan into action and fast, there's no time to waste, number one on the list, Val Crowe's Village Shop. Max, grab your lunch box we'll need somewhere to put the snake if we can catch it. Lucy grab your school bag, we'll need something to put Max's lunch box in, Spag Bol...."

"Yelp," yapped Spag Bol, who was now hiding under the sofa. "Spag Bol, stay here and guard the house, if anyone calls or knocks at the door, especially Lady Lavender or anyone from the Pumperton Paper, just tell them, we have all... we have all gone to the seaside."

"Woof!"

Panic!

The Pumperton Paper must have landed on the doormat of every villager in Pumperton, because there was panic everywhere. Villagers were running up the high street, down the high street, along the high street, even around in circles on the high street.

A traffic jam stretched from one end of

Pumperton to the other with people who had decided the safest option was to leave the village until the snake had been found. At the post office a queue of people were buying its entire supply of bubble-wrap and parcel tape.

"I'm going to seal up my letter-box and windows, no snake will be able to get me!" said one man, while another wrapped himself up in bubble wrap mumbling something about maximum protection.

Parcel tape!

Grandma Bendy, Max and Lucy, who were on their way to Val Crowe's Village Shop, couldn't believe how silly everyone was being.

"Don't they know that the paper makes most of it up, Grandma?" asked Lucy.

"People have short memories my dear, they've clearly forgotten about last summer," said Grandma Bendy.

Last summer the Pumperton Paper wrote this...

THE PUMPERTON PAPER

IT'S JUMPER-TOWN IN PUMPERTON AS SUMMER SNOW STORMS IN!

Everyone in the village started wearing woolly jumpers, hats, scarves, gloves, and Wellington boots. Some dads in the village wore woolly tights under their trousers, while mums put on sheepskin underwear. In August!

It was 25°C, hot and sunny and the people of Pumperton were sweating under six layers of woolly winter clothing, absolutely delighted at their cleverness. They'd say to each other

sheepskin knickers!!

Woolly tights!

things like, "Gosh, this heat! I can't bear it - but we'll all be laughing when that snow storm hits any day now."

The Pumperton Paper later had to issue an apology admitting they had been wrong, but only after two elderly ladies in thick duffel coats, mittens, hats, ski boots and goggles were taken to hospital for overheating. And

emergency !!

now, the villagers were believing the
Pumperton Paper again.

"They'll believe anything they read," said
Grandma Bendy zigzagging her way through
the crowds of panicking people.
Val Crowe's Village Shop was at the far end of
the high street and was the nearest shop to
the school, so it was an obvious first place to
look for the snake.

The village shop wasn't quite what you'd
expect from a little shop next to a school. It
didn't sell sweets, crisps, fizzy drinks or
chocolate, not even weird tasting cooking
chocolate. In fact there was nothing in the

village shop you would like to eat. Instead, it was full of things grown-ups pretended they liked to eat - even though they too would prefer a gooey chocolate bar.

stale pineapple cubes

Things like lentils, mung beans and little hessian sacks filled with dried stale cubes of pineapple and brightly coloured knitted hats that came free with every green sludge smoothie. So it wouldn't be surprising if the snake had gone unnoticed among the strange packets of food on the shelves.
"Dring!" rang the bell above the shop

Tibetan Lentils

Mung Beans

Knitted hats + socks

SMOOTH CABBAGE

SMOOTH PARSNIP + BEET

SMOOTH NETTLE + CHIVE

disgustin smoothie

door as Grandma Bendy, Lucy and Max entered. No-one was there, but then came the

**'thud
thud
thud'**

Totally bonkers!

of Val Crowe running down the stairs wearing what looked like knitted running gear.

"Oh my giddy goodness! For a moment I thought you were the snake ha

ha ha!" said Val in a high-pitched voice as she stopped at the foot of the stairs with a basket in one hand and a recorder in the other.

Lucy and Max shared an amused look; Val like the other villagers had clearly gone mad.

"I was going to charm you... with this," she said, waving the recorder at them. "Well not you, but the snake, but you're not the snake, so panic over, ha ha. Come in, come in, but shut the door, shut it quickly!" said Val, running and slamming the door shut herself.

Val Crowe lived upstairs and ran the shop; in fact, she 'ran' everywhere. No matter what the weather: rain, hail, sleet, snow or blizzards, Val Crowe would be running in it.

"Lentils!" Val suddenly cried out, "You're here for lentils! I knew it as soon as I saw you," and

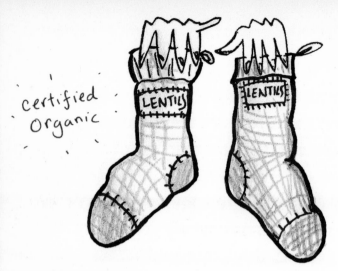

certified
Organic

before Grandma Bendy had time to answer, Val ran over to the lentil section and began holding up different packets to show them.

"You're in luck, I have twenty-two different types of lentils fresh in today and these ones come in an organic sock! Buy two and not only do you have plenty of lentils, but a lovely toasty pair of socks for your feet, just in time for winter, isn't that fabulous?!" she said excitedly.

Grandma Bendy didn't really want to let Val know they were actually here on some very

important snake finding business, so agreed
to buy one sock of lentils, then asked, "Would
it be ok, if we just browsed?"

"Yes, yes of course, browse away, that corner
is very good for browsing, we've just
had a delivery of three hundred
and sixty seven types of dried
leaves to make tea with,"
replied Val, "I'll just be over
here, if you have any questions, just shout
and I'll be with you in a jiffy."

Yaks
wool

With Val Crowe out of the way, Grandma
Bendy, Max and Lucy were free to look for the
snake.

"Max, look under the shelves and along the
floor. Lucy, look along the middle shelves and
I'll look up here," instructed
Grandma Bendy.

← Hessian
sack

ORGANIC FROGS & FROG FEET £4.99 + £2

Grandma Bendy twizzled her arms along the very tops of the shelves between the hessian sacks of dried satsuma skins and the bags of organic frogs.

Lucy searched between the rows of lentil socks, the packets of tree bark, the thick organic woolly underpants and inside the Papier-Mâché Wellington boots. *keeps your bottom warm*

Max searched under the shelves, in between the gaps in the floorboards and in a large basket that was full of Tibetan yak wool.

"Nothing here," said Max, looking puzzled at the wool.

"Or here," said Lucy.

"Flubbersticks, nothing here either," replied Bendy.

"Right, no faffing, next is the churchyard and there's no time to waste, it'll be dark soon," said Grandma Bendy.

So they paid Val for her sock of lentils and left the shop.

The churchyard was across the road from Val Crowe's shop, the sun was already low in the sky and had started to cast long shadows across the ground, making everything look that little bit spookier. Luckily, because it was a Monday, the church itself was shut so they only had the churchyard to search.

"I think we should all stay together this time," said Bendy.

"Phew," said Max.

They walked slowly around the churchyard together, step-by-step, following Grandma Bendy closely. Lucy started to feel a little bit scared as they walked around the gravestones and was extra careful not to step on top of any.

They looked left to right and right to left as

they walked, through the long grass and along the pebble paths between the gravestones and by the time they'd walked around the whole churchyard, the sun had set.

"G-G-Grandma, can we maybe just go home now?" asked Max looking around nervously in the dark.

"Really? But we are just getting started Maxy,"
replied Bendy.

"Actually Grandma," said Lucy reaching out to
hold Grandma Bendy's hand,
"I think I'd like to go home now too."

"You kids these days, a little darkness didn't
harm any.... woah!"

A bat swooped low over their heads nearly hitting them.

"Yikes! You're right, let's skedaddle out of here!" said Grandma Bendy changing her mind very quickly and she shot off faster than Val Crowe can run, pulling Max and Lucy along with her.

A pretty scary bat attack!

Yikes!!

The search continues

Grandma Bendy was already wide-awake when her alarm went off the next morning. Neither she nor Spag Bol had slept very well and, by the sound of the screams that had echoed around the village throughout the night, neither had anyone else.

'DRIIIING DRIIIING DRIIIING!!'

SMACK,

CRASH,

THUD!

Grandma Bendy hit her alarm clock knocking it to the floor.

"Morning, Spag-Bol," she chimed.

Spag Bol, who was still very tired, opened his little mouth for a big yawn, stretched his front paws and jumped up onto Grandma Bendy's bed to lick her face.

Grandma Bendy got up and slid down the banister then went to make a nice cup of tea with some multi-coloured sprinkles on top. Spag Bol was just polishing off his favourite food ever, spaghetti bolognese, when there

Do NOT try at home!

was a familiar knock at the door.

"Woof woof," Spag Bol wagged his tail and ran around in circles with excitement, then darted towards the front door to greet Lucy and Max.

Grandma Bendy sipped her cup of tea and crunched on the sprinkles, and twizzled her arm down the corridor to let them in.

"Morning Spag Bol, morning Grandma," sang Lucy and Max.

"C'mon on through," shouted Bendy down the corridor. "There's tea and toast, and toast in tea if you want it, but let's all be quick, we've searching to do and plans to commence! Next on our list is the park and the playground...

No crusts!

tea

tea

now I can see what you're thinking, trying to find a snake in a park is going to be tricky. Well yes you're right, but I have a plan up my sleeve!" exclaimed Bendy, "What I don't have a plan for is that pesky goose who seems to think he owns the park, but we'll just have to wing that part. Let's go..."

But just as they were ready to leave they heard the Pumperton Paper drop through the letterbox with the latest headline:

> **Three hundred and fifty three thousand snake sightings overnight. Zero confirmed. Hundreds of calls made to our snake hotline (0555 555 555).**
>
> **Today we ask, is there more than one snake?**
>
> **Police urge: "Stay Safe. Stay indoors. If you see a snake call the snake hotline."**

"What utter rubbish," said Bendy, "More than one snake, how ridiculous!" Grandma Bendy was about to throw the paper away, when she noticed an advert at the bottom of the page.

SSSSSSSSSSSSCREWBALLS

KNICKER BOA-CONSTRICTOR GLORY's

99's WITH A SNAKE

Jelly Snakes Galore!

IT'S ICE CREAM TO SCREAM ABOUT
ONLY AT
MR BRAIN FREEZE'S
ICE CREAM PARLOUR

WHILE STOCKS LAST

"Look, my snake searching swat team!" said Bendy, holding up the advert to Lucy and Max. "If there's any left by the time we get down there, it's my treat! Spag Bol, we'll bring you some back, we promise, although it might melt a little."

"Woof!"

"But first, to the park," said Grandma Bendy. They left the house and as Grandma Bendy shut the door she waved goodbye to Spag Bol. They walked down the garden path and noticed that Lady Lavender's house looked a little different today...

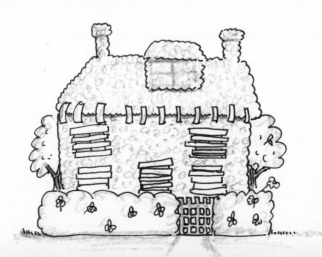

Pumperton High Street was nothing at all like
it had been yesterday afternoon. There were
no people dashing around panicking, no
traffic jams, no queues at the post office, in
fact there was no-one on the high street at all.
Grandma Bendy was rather happy about this,
with no-one to disturb them it would make
their snake searching mission much quicker.
They walked past Val Crowe's Village Shop,
past the church and into the park, without
seeing anyone.

It was strange seeing the park with no-one in
it, it looked even bigger than usual.

"Tumbleweed"

"We'll never get to Mr Brain Freeze's," sighed Max, looking across the vast space of parkland.

"It's probably going to take maybe forever to search all of this," said Lucy.

"C'mon my little search team, your clever Grandma has thought about this already," said Bendy. "Even for someone with these long bendy legs, it would take an age, let alone you little nippers, so I wasn't planning on searching the park on foot!"

"If not by foot, by what?" asked Max puzzled.

"Wait and see Maxy, now all good search teams should be well prepared," said Bendy.

Grandma Bendy reached into her backpack and pulled out three telescopes of varying sizes.

"This one's for you. This is yours and this one is for me," she said, handing them out.

Grandma Bendy then pulled out the map of the park and a pen.

"We'll start here at the bandstand, then we'll go

this way, then back that way, around here, up here and then finally down to the lake," Bendy drew the route on the map.

"I need you to be eagle-eyed through your spy-glasses, okay?"

"But how are we going to go OVER the lake?" asked Lucy staring at the route Grandma Bendy had drawn on the map.

"When we get to the bandstand, you will see!" said Bendy.

"This is still going to take forever," sighed Max again.

The launch

The bandstand was right in the middle of the park. It was long rather than round like usual bandstands and had a sloping roof. It was very old and in need of a good lick of paint. When they arrived at it, Max couldn't believe what he saw. On the roof was a hang-glider.

"Are we... are we... going in that!?" asked Max excitedly.

"Of course we are, how else do you propose we search this vast space of parkland if not from above!" said Grandma Bendy.

"But how did you get it?" asked Lucy, totally gobsmacked.

"Friends in high places my dear, now no more questions, we must get going while the wind is still up." said Bendy.

Grandma Bendy picked Max up and lifted him onto the bandstand's roof, then did the same with Lucy, before stretching her arms up and climbing up herself.

"Now remember, spy-glasses to the ground at

all times, if you see anything that
looks like Boris, then shout loudly,
it may be hard to hear up there.
Oh and most importantly,
hold on tight!"

Grandma Bendy
fastened the safety
belts around Lucy and Max,
then took hold of the hang-
glider and ran as fast as her
bendy legs could from one
end of the bandstand to the
other. As they reached the
edge, the hang-glider
caught the wind and
zoomed up into the air until
they were soaring high
above the trees.

Up, up, up
and away

"Engage spy-glasses," shouted Bendy.

They looked through their telescopes to the park below as they flew over the bandstand, then up towards the rugby fields then around to the outer edges of the park. They'd been up in the air for almost an hour, when they changed direction towards the lake.

"I can't see anything," shouted Lucy.

"Keep searching, look for movement," shouted Grandma Bendy.

"Oh no!" shouted Max, "The goose!" he pointed as they swooped towards the lake. He took a closer look through his telescope and saw the goose staring straight back at him. It didn't look very happy.

"Erm, Grandma? I think it's spotted us," he said.

"It's taking off, Grandma!" shouted Lucy in a panic.

The wind was carrying them towards the lake and the goose had already begun flapping its wings hard.

"Don't fret, just hold on tight," shouted Grandma Bendy, looking a little worried herself. The goose was climbing higher and higher, catching them up.

"I think it's chasing us!" shouted Lucy.

"No, no, don't be so silly," reassured Grandma Bendy.

"HONK HONK!"
screeched the goose as it chased the glider.

"Ok, yes it is!" shouted Bendy back.

"HONK HONK HONK,"
screeched the goose again. It was now almost level with them.

"It's angry," said Max.

"Hold on tight," shouted Grandma Bendy, she swerved to the left and then quickly to the right.

But it was no good, the goose was far too
quick and it was right on their tail, trying
to bite Grandma Bendy's toes with its beak.

"Team Snake Search to abort search mission,"
shouted Grandma Bendy.

The goose was trying to chase them out of the
park altogether. Bendy knew she had to
distract it, then she remembered the sock of
lentils.

With one arm on the glider she twizzled her
other arm around to her backpack, pulled out
the lentil sock and handed it straight to Lucy.

"On three!" shouted Grandma Bendy.
Lucy looked at the lentils in her hand and
realised exactly what Grandma Bendy wanted
to her do; she just hoped she wouldn't miss.

"One..." shouted Grandma Bendy and Lucy pulled her arm back and took aim.

"Two..." Lucy shut one eye for accuracy.

"Three!" Bendy yelled and Lucy threw the sock with all her might, knocking the goose right on its beak and sending it flapping in another direction.

"HONK HONK HONK!" it screeched angrily as it flew off course. The glider then swooped into a dive.

"Aaargh!" screamed Max and Lucy as their tummies jumped into their mouths.

"Look out, coming into land," shouted Bendy, but Max and Lucy had their eyes firmly shut.

81 Thwack!

"Woooooaaaaah, here we gooooo!" They
swerved to the right, then left, then the right
again and landed with a bump.

With the wind no longer rushing through their
hair or swooshing past their ears, everything
seemed so quiet. A
distant "honk
honk" broke
the
silence
high

above them. The goose, having chased them out of the park, was now flying back towards the lake with the sock of lentils in its beak.

Grandma Bendy wondered if it would be the first to actually enjoy eating something from Val Crowe's shop.

"Phewy," sighed Grandma Bendy climbing out of the glider and unfastening all the safety straps. "What a ride! Everyone okay? Lucy? Maxy? Okay?"

Max nodded and gave a slightly shaky thumbs up, while Lucy climbed out of the glider with her legs wobbling like jelly.

"I think we can tick the park off the list," said Grandma Bendy pulling out her notebook and drawing a line through the park and playground.

"And can you believe where we've landed? What luck! What a landing! I knew I still had it in me!"

Once they had all had a moment or two to recover, Max looked up and grinned a huge grin as he realised where they were.

"Mr Brain Freeze's Ice Cream Parlour! And it's still open!"

Mr Brainfreeze's Ice Cream Parlour

Unlike everywhere else in Pumperton today, Mr Brain Freeze's Ice Cream Parlour was extremely busy. Almost the whole of Horace Hicks First School were there, it was buzzing with excited children.

Slurrrrp, slurp

On the picnic benches outside children slurped and tinkered their spoons against ice cream glasses and occasionally a cry of

"Aaaaarrrrrrrrrrrhhhhhh!

ICE CREAM

HEADACHE!"

could be heard.

Brain Freeze was certainly making the most of the 'Great Snake Escape'. Some might say 'cashing in' but the children didn't care. Spoonfuls of ice cream with squeezy chocolate sauce were far better than sitting in a lesson of double maths with boring Mr

'fractions are fun' Peterson.

"Last on the list!" exclaimed Grandma Bendy, "It has to be here!"

But the ice cream parlour was so busy, it was going to be difficult to search for anything. At least a class full of children were inside at any one time.

"Can I have a 99 with a snake and blood sauce?" asked Max, "Please," he added, almost forgetting.

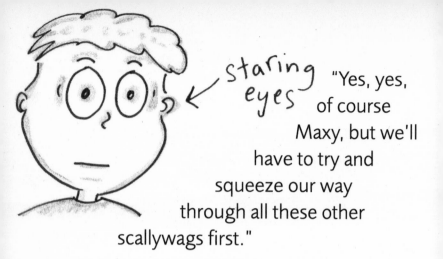

staring eyes ←

"Yes, yes, of course Maxy, but we'll have to try and squeeze our way through all these other scallywags first."

Lucy didn't know if she liked being at the parlour. She was sure some of the children were staring at her and was doubly sure they were talking about her. It made her realise, they had to find the snake and reunite it with

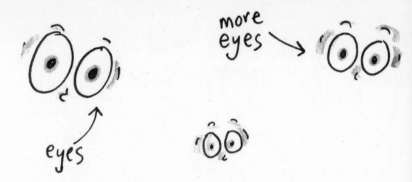

more
eyes →

eyes →

Mike quickly, so everyone would know it wasn't her fault.

But the parlour was last on the list and if it wasn't there, they may never find it.

Grandma Bendy noticed Lucy looked worried, so she reached out, put her arm around her and hugged her close.

"Just ignore them, they haven't got guts or brains like you and I bet none of them have

Big → glare

been chased by a goose while looking for a snake through a spy-glass and flying a hang-glider over a park," whispered Bendy in Lucy's ear.

Lucy chuckled. It sounded bonkers, but it was true and she did feel pretty proud of herself even if it was all a bit mad.

"What ice cream would you like?" asked Grandma Bendy.

"Um… I think just a normal, non-snake one please," said Lucy.

Lucy, Max and Grandma Bendy stood at the back of the queue, which stretched all the way outside the parlour, but it didn't seem too long before they made their way inside.

JELLY SNAKE | FIZZY SNAKES | SNAKEY SNAKES | SLIMEY SNAKES | SNAK SWIR

Mr Brain Freeze had really gone to town decorating the parlour with snakes, not real snakes of course, but jelly snakes. There was a giant jelly snake hung from one side of the ceiling to the other. Two more giant jelly snakes spiralled down the pillars and there were hundreds of mini jelly snakes decorating the walls.

Along the back wall of the parlour Mr Brain Freeze had pretty much every type of sweet

MINTY MAHEM | FLYING SAUCER | VANILLA WITH DOTS | C T.

you could imagine, it was like a giant pick 'n' mix stand filled with sweets from floor to ceiling and the ice cream counter itself could hold up to fifty flavours.

Behind the counter Mr Brain Freeze danced as he served the ice cream. Even from the back of the busy parlour you could see his crazy ice cream style hair bouncing around on top of his head and you could hear him singing...

"I know it's a squish and a bit of a squeeze, but it's well worth the wait for a Mr Brain Freeze. Don't push, don't shove, you'll be in like a breeze, be ready to order, but don't forget to say please!"

Just then Lucy heard a familiar voice at the counter.

"Give me a 99 with a snake and lots of blood sauce," said the voice.

"And?" said Mr Brain Freeze.

"That's it, I want a 99 with a snake and lots of blood sauce," demanded the voice again.

"Jeez! I think you're forgetting to say the magic 'P' word," said Mr Brain Freeze again.

"Humph," sighed the voice impatiently, then continued, "A 99, a snake and lots of blood sauce with the magic P word 'PLEASE!'"

It was Mike! And as usual he'd left his manners at home. Lucy didn't really want to see Mike, so she stuck close to Grandma Bendy at the back of the queue.

"Of course, coming up, oh please, I just tease," sang Mr Brain Freeze. Mr Brain Freeze took a cone and placed two scoops of vanilla ice cream, one scoop of bright green lime ice cream, then covered it in raspberry blood sauce until it dripped down the cone. He then turned to the sweet wall and scooped up a green stripy jelly snake and was about to place it on top of Mike's ice cream when....

"AAAAAAAAAAAAHHH

The children at the front of the queue screamed and started pushing and shoving each other away from the counter. Mr Brain Freeze was puzzled, he didn't know what all the commotion was about, so started singing a line of his song again...

"Don't push, don't shove and you'll be in like a breeze, it's worth the wait, for a...."

But the children wouldn't stop screaming.

"What on earth is going on?" he shouted.

The snake

Mike was puzzled too, he was getting pushed and shoved in all directions and was getting really impatient for his ice cream. He reached to snatch his ice cream out of Mr Brain Freeze's hands when he realised why everyone was screaming.

NOT a happy face!

"Boris!!!" he shouted, "BORIS, you're okay!"

Mr Brain Freeze, who was still baffled, followed the direction of Mike's gaze to his own hand and an icy shiver ran down his spine. He wasn't holding a green and yellow jelly snake, he was holding a real snake and it was trying to wiggle up his arm.

"Ahhhhh!" screamed Mr Brain Freeze, immediately dropping the snake.

"Grandma, quick, do something," shouted Lucy who had witnessed everything from the back of the parlour.

Boris was on the floor somewhere, but so were fifty-two children's feet trying to run and jump away from the snake. Grandma Bendy decided the only way to get through the crowd was by crawling through the sea of legs across the floor.

"Go Grandma!" shouted Lucy and Max, trying to stand back from the pushing crowds.

Grandma Bendy knelt down and began carefully crawling her way to the front of the

parlour, zigzagging this way, then that way,
through the moving legs, missing one child
then bumping into the next.

"Where are you Mr Snakey?" called Grandma
Bendy to Boris. She wriggled her way around
the legs getting closer and closer to the front
of the parlour, when she spotted the snake
slithering away from her.

But she wasn't the only one on the floor trying
to catch Boris.

"Boris, Boris, it's me, Mike, Boris come here, come home!"

There were at least twenty-two pairs of legs between Grandma Bendy and Boris when she saw Mike just an arm's length away from reaching the snake. She didn't have a second to lose, she shot out her arm, stretching and twizzling it through the legs in front of her, twisting to the left, then to the right, twizzling through the middle, as far as she possibly could and just as Mike had his fingertips on

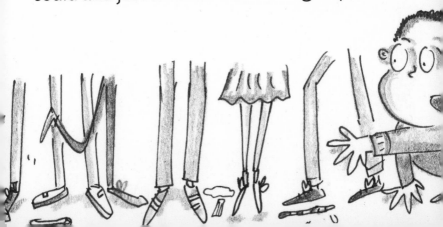

Boris, she grabbed it and let her stretchy bendy arm ping straight back to her, like an elastic band.

'Ping!'

Grandma Bendy stood up, holding Boris triumphantly in the air high above everyone's heads.

"One stripey, green and yellow snake!

Maxy, lunchbox, quick!" yelled Grandma Bendy.

Max ran over and opened his lunchbox and just as Grandma Bendy was about to place the snake into it, a bright white light flashed in their faces. A camera flash! And the person with the camera was Suzy Valentine, reporter to the Pumperton Paper.

SNAP!!

"Uh oh," said Grandma

Bendy, placing the snake into the lunchbox then shutting the lid safely.

"Gotcha," winked Suzy Valentine then dashed off towards the front of the parlour.

The remaining children in the parlour stopped screaming and pushing and looked towards Mike. He looked a mess, not only was he covered in ice cream, sprinkles and sauce, but he was crying.

Lucy couldn't believe she was seeing Mike Grimace, big bully of Horace Hicks First School actually crying and she felt a little sorry for him.

"Please," he sobbed, "please can I just have Boris back?"

"Now this is good!" exclaimed Suzy Valentine, jotting down everything being said in a notebook, she lifted up her camera to take a photo of Mike, but Grandma Bendy stood in her way.

"He's my best friend," sobbed Mike again, "he's not dangerous or anything."

Grandma Bendy waved at Lucy to come over. Lucy stood in front of Mike, now feeling very sorry for him.

"Max will give you Boris back, if you just tell everyone the truth," said Lucy to Mike.

Mike sniffed and nodded and turned to Suzy Valentine, who was now holding a recording machine and a microphone and pointing it at Mike.

"Boris is mine, it was me," he said, "I was the one who brought Boris into school and please, I just want him back."

"Now that's a scoop!" chirped Suzy Valentine winking at Mr Brain Freeze, who had only just reappeared from hiding behind the counter. And then out of nowhere, Sergeant Nevil Rodent walked into the parlour.

"'Ello, 'ello, disturbance at the parlour, eh?" Grandma Bendy explained the last ten minutes of chaos to Sergeant Nevil Rodent, who listened, nodded, hummed and ahhed, then looked very relieved.

"So the snake has been found and this young lady is in the clear," said the sergeant, tapping Lucy on the shoulder. "Well, you'll be pleased to hear I have spoken to Mrs McDotty and she doesn't want any more trouble, so Master Grimace, you can have your snake back, but only if you sign this agreement to promise everyone that you'll keep Boris safely at home," said Sergeant Rodent and he handed Mike a piece of paper to sign.

"Another case solved!" he added, looking very pleased with himself as if he had solved the whole case himself.

"Here you go Mike," said Lucy handing over Max's lunchbox with Boris inside. Mike sniffed and then smiled at Lucy and for a moment, they were almost, sort of, nearly, friends.

Back to normal...
almost

With the snake no longer on the loose, Horace Hicks would reopen tomorrow and the people of Pumperton could begin taking all the bubble wrap and tape off their windows and letterboxes and come out of hiding.

Max, Lucy and Grandma Bendy walked home slurping their ice creams, it had been a very eventful day. As they turned the corner into Grandma Bendy's street, they noticed a very grumpy looking Lady Lavender unwrapping the bubble wrap from around her house. With

all the chaos over with and Lucy in the clear,
Lady Lavender would have to find something
else to gossip about.

As Grandma Bendy opened the door a very
excited Spag Bol greeted them.

"Woof woof," he barked.

"Oh, I didn't forget Spag Bol," said Grandma

Bendy and she walked through to the kitchen and poured out a flask of melted Ice Cream Tuesdae into his bowl.

They all sat down exhausted, but before they could relax the familiar sound of the letterbox rattled.

"Well that was quick!" said Grandma Bendy, recognising the unmistakeable thud of the

Pumperton Paper landing on the doormat. She stretched her arm down the hallway to get it and brought it back to the table, where they all could see it.

> **People of Pumperton relax! The snake has been found and it turns out it wasn't dangerous at all. Hero Mrs G Bendy of 22 Cucumber Close caught the snake in Mr Brain Freeze's Ice Cream Parlour.**
>
> **No-one was harmed. The snake named 'Boris' has now been reunited with its owner.**
>
> **Class 4B girl was NOT to blame.**

"Wow, you're on the front page!" said Max.

"And they've called you a hero!" said Lucy.

"Utter nonsense! You can't believe what you read in the Pumperton Paper!" said Grandma

Bendy looking embarrassed, but rather pleased.

"Besides, I couldn't have done anything without my scallywags!" she said and she turned over the page of the paper, to see this…

THIS DIARY BELONGS TO:

Spag Bol

↑
mini me

Private

Keep out

"Spag Bol stay here and guard the house, if anyone calls or knocks at the door, especially Lady Lavender or anyone from the Pumperton Paper, just tell them, we have all... we have all gone to the seaside!"

Ooh, the seaside! 🖤 I love the seaside.

But the snake! **Eek!** I don't love the snake.

Hmmm... I'll get the bus to Sandysocks Seaside! 🐶

Grrr... What do I need?

Bucket ✓   Spade ✓ 🖤
Shorts ✓   Suncream ✓
Sunglasses ✓   🐶

Off I go to SANDYSOCKS! How though?
Ooh, on the No. 92 Bus.

Vroom, vroom. *Woohoo! Weeeeeee!*

ticket

Ooh! We're here!

WELCOME to

SANDYSOCKS

Look at the sand!

And the sunshine! Woof!

And the sea! Woof, woof!

What to do first? I'll dig a hole, and another, and another!

Oh look! I found a shoe! I'll take it in the sea.

Hmm, where did it go? Never mind.

Splish, splash, splosh! Ooh, fishes! Grr, woof, woof!

slimey
Seaweed

That was fun. Maybe I'll dig another hole...
Ooh look a crab!

Let's play! Grrr, grrr, woof, woof! **Gotcha!**

OOH, A STICK!

Here, little, old lady. You can play with the crab. I'll just pop him in your lap.

I love sticks. But it's really quite hot now...
I would love an...

Ice cream! An ice cream van, perfect!

"Excuse me, woof. Could I, grr, have an ice cream. Woof?"

Hmmm, maybe he didn't hear me?

"One, woof. Ice, grrr, cream! Please!"

No, I don't think he speaks english.

Oh look, a nice, old man! He'll understand.

"Grr, hello. Can I, woof, have an ice cream?"

YAY! Result! Ice-cream!

Lick, slurp, yum!

"Thank you, woof!"

Ahh, I love the seaside.

Sandysocks
shell

Oh no! Look at the time! To the bus!

Vroooom. Woohoo! Weeeeeee!

WELCOME
to

PUMPERTON

Home! Phew! Wait, who's that?

"Grrrrrrrrr, woof! Go away, Lady Lavender!"

Yes! Job well done.

Oh, the door! "Woof, woof, woof!"

Bendy!

Max and Lucy!

And an ice-cream for me, yay! Best day ever.

MORE ice-cream!

Spag Bol